Nomad Moon

Stories by
Doug Mathewson

Edited by
Sally Reno

Červená Barva Press
Somerville, Massachusetts

Červená Barva Press
P.O. Box 440357
W. Somerville, MA 02144-3222

www.cervenabarvapress.com

Bookstore: www.thelostbookshelf.com

Cover photo: Doug Mathewson

Author photo: Gemma Mathewson

Cover design: William J. Kelle

ISBN: 978-1-950063-56-7

ACKNOWLEDGMENTS

Original Publication Credits:

Battered Suitcase, "Twenty One Guns"

Blink-Ink, "Inky," "Curbside"

The Boston Literary Magazine, "The Muse," "Faadan," (appearing under a different title) "Summer Satisfaction," "Reprieve," "Come Spring," "Safe Harbor," "Senior Momentum," "Crossing the Hudson"

Dog Plotz, "Bus Station"

Full of Crow Press, "Bread Knife"

Ginosko Literary Review, "Watching the Seasons"

Kitty Wang's American Gazette, "Elvie"

Little 2 Say, "Family Album," "Farm Stand," "Missed Connections," "Man From Mars"

Pen Pricks Micro Fiction, "The Muse"

Poetry Pacific, "Karaoke"

Postcards, Poems & Prose, "Fall Colors"

Six Sentences, "Early Call"

Virtual Verse, "Greenpoint"

Special thanks to Sally Reno for editing this collection.
My sincere thanks to Gloria Mindock of Červená Barva Press.

Thank you also to all of the editors who originally published these stories, especially Robin Stratton, Editor of *The Boston Literary Magazine*.

TABLE OF CONTENTS

For Gemma

"When you rock and roll with me ...."

Nomad Moon

Inky

After an alarming number of rapid twitchy side to side glances, Isabella spoke. "This is such an *Inky* story" she nervously whispered, switching personas. It was only then I noticed she had somehow enameled playing cards on all of her teeth. Spades on the top, and hearts on the bottom.

The Muse

I saw The Muse last night at the 24-hour corner store and she looked like shit. She was buying cigarettes and Slim Jims, I was getting cat food and a Slurpee. Poor thing, she had on an old bathrobe over her house coat, a bomber hat with ear flaps, and men's shoes.

Kid behind the counter told her she couldn't smoke in the store. I said something. I said "don't say that," or "leave her the fuck alone" or "she's alright" or something. I don't know, but I said something. She ground it out on the linoleum and paid. On her way out she touched my arm and whispered "I haven't forgotten, you Bunny."

Grape Arbor

My grandfather didn't speak much English but we got along. We would sit in the grape arbors shade. He would say "now we smoke." From the pocket of his huge pants came a can of Bugler tobacco. He would roll two cigarettes and we would smoke in silence, just enjoying being together. I was nine.

Faadah

My rock caught him above the eye.
He called me a "little fucker,"
said he'd kill me.
I screamed back,
"catch me first, asshole,"
Then he threw a rock,
hard and fast, almost got me!
Not bad.
So far new Priest seems okay.

Family Album

We never had a family album, it wasn't our style. No photos of picnics or birthdays, no graduations, Easter Bonnets or Christmas Mornings. We had a family envelope. That's how we were I guess. Our envelope was tattered and old filled mostly without dated papers and useless receipts. Hardly any pictures or clippings.

When Mom died and the newspaper needed a photo for her obituary we cut their wedding picture in half. When Dad passed on two years later we couldn't find his half! The best we could do was his driver's license. Too bad it had "Suspended DWI" stamped across his face.

And wouldn't you know it? Now the darn dog's gone missing and not picture one of the old mutt! We'll just have to use a picture of somebody else's dog for the "Missing" posters. Have ya seen him? :(

Summer Satisfaction

workday morning late again
old convertible my summer ride
muffler loud, radio louder
sets off the boss's car alarm

Farm Stand

The first summer I didn't go back home I worked at a farm stand near Augusta. Things were different down there in what was south for me. Back home was so far north what we got on TV was all in French.

The sign out front said "Farm Fresh & Native Grown." There was this guy, drove up, wanted to know if the grapefruit was locally grown. Claude La Croix, he was from up north too, shakes his head a little and says "no sir, been a bad year for grapefruit around here, these came from New Hampshire."

I still laugh now. Back home lying was a sin, but we wasn't back home.

Twenty One Guns

That Army bus was a small one, just enough room for the eight of us and our gear. It was hotter than the Devil's own oven in the summer, freezing in the winter, and leaked both spring and fall. I lived inside that olive drab shell for better than two full years with the rest of the Honor Guard as we bumped and wound over and back the Appalachians through West Virginia, Virginia, and Tennessee. War was what keep us busy those years '67, '68, and part of '69. We took turns driving, those of us who knew how, but when we got to our stop it was always Larry who played Taps and presented the flag to the family. The rest of us stood at attention, after we each fired three times. Then Larry, horn under his arm, would salute and give who-ever the folded flag. Then we'd drive to the next one. Little towns mostly, some places not even towns at all. Soldiers families tried real hard to be strong and proud for their boy, for their country.

I turned eighteen on that bus, nineteen too, and we gave out must have been better than a thousand flags. Didn't keep one. Didn't keep anything really, just my boots (them being the only shoes I had). Other guys on the bus, them GI's, came and went, and I left in my time too. Went back my old job, or near enough. Still workin' Dairy Queen. Just mostly on the grille now, only mop-up weekday nights. I see kids come in, no older than we was. Always hungry after the game or a school play. I think, well maybe where I was those Vietnam years was like a school play. I wished so hard the dead boys would come in from the wings, pushin' each other and taking their bows. The broken hearted girls smiling now, holding roses.

Watching the Seasons

Him being more your uncle than mine, you're close kin and me only poor relations, I thought it best you talk first when he began about his property, leaving a will, what would happen to the land.

Imagine you'd be thinking about horses. You always been talking about them since you were little. Playing horses. Dreaming horses. Talking horses and living on a farm.

I wasn't thinking about anything. Coming back and Janie being gone. I didn't like to think about past or future, they both hurt, so I left them alone.

We signed up together right after she got out of high school. I was a year behind and quit. So we were GI Joe and GI Jane. Come back in a couple of years, have some money, get a place. Maybe she'd go to school. I'd need a job, farm on the side for us. We coulda been a commercial on the TV. High school sweethearts off to war, except Janie got killed. Some fool Lieutenant got them all blown up and not half of her come home. Not from the weight of that government rubber bag. Knew you'd take more than you should from your uncle, but not in a thieving way. More than your share, is all. You best move in now. Learn your way around, and no lie, he needs the help.

I'll stay on, you want. Keep to myself, and watch the seasons. Hard sometimes, trying to forget and remember at the same time.

Fall Colors

Coming up from behind it wasn't until the car was close that I noticed the figure walking ahead was wearing a saffron robe. A muted curry color that stood out from the fall foliage more by shape than color. A few miles away is a Buddhist retreat center so he wasn't entirely out of place on this back road in western Massachusetts. He wore a large backpack. On one side it had a vertical sleeve for his full sized umbrella. I very much wanted to imagine it was a sword.

Early Call

She called me from the Tibetan boarder on a phone she borrowed from an Israeli tourist. Said she been to a temple in the mountains. The temple cats all wore earrings and she thought of me. I smiled all day thinking about that early call. I'm not a cat and I don't wear earrings. She called because she loves me and that made me happier than the fattest cat with the fanciest earrings of all.

Reprieve

Unexpected early dismissal from jury duty
left me on my own
midday midweek midtown
used book store cafe near the court tantalized me in
juror parking was free so I still had ten bucks
clerk with race-car tattoos and vertical hair
took six of my dollars
for a poetry book and a scone
scone was pear and almonds
book was Richard Garcia
both were great
reading and eating in a sunny spot
playing out my own alternate lives
with sailor me lost at sea
when cowboy me moved to town
disco me died too young
astronaut me who never took off
royal me without a throne
monastic me who suffered alone
the afternoon was passing
time to head home
the evening was still open
for us to decide who to be

Greenpoint

On the bus to New York she made a dozen lists, and changed each one a dozen times. On the plane to New York he made dozen lists, and changed each one a dozen times. Always first on her list was a knife. A good sharp knife and she'd use it too if that bastard (or anyone else) came after her. Always first on his list was a knife. A good sharp knife, that's the first thing you need in a kitchen his grandmother had taught him. Overhead was her duffel. The few clothes she could grab, and of course her iguanas Peaches and Herb. Overhead was his duffel. The few clothes he owned worth taking, and of course his drawings and a books. Dozing she thought of the husband she left, how he hit her one time too many. She could still picture him, drunk, breathing heavy, belt doubled in his hand. She ran. Dozing he thought of his grandmother, all she taught him, the heart break of her death. He could still picture her, with her short orange hair, smoking a little home made cigar, and walking her old iguana Judas on his leash. He couldn't stay. Off the bus from Texas she found a cheap Brooklyn rent. Off the plane from Ecuador he found a cheap Brooklyn rent. She cut her hair short, to look like a city girl, dyed it woodpecker red. He cut off his long braid, to look like an American, saved it wrapped in tissue. She took what work she could, wouldn't file for aid. He took what work he could, visa long expired. Hot summer night. She's on the fire escape, smoking what she rolled, hunting knife, cutting up bananas for Herbie in her lap. Hot summer night. He's on the fire escape, lemon soda, chef's knife, cutting up plantains to fry for dinner.

Knives in hand their eyes meet. She smiles, then smiles again. He seems nice. "My Christ," he whispers, what a beautiful woman....... She reminds me of someone."

Missed Connections:

You - Three thousand dollar stroller, and sleeping child.

Me - Six hundred dollar car and someone else's dog.

The light changed, I rev'd the engine, you flipped me off.
I blew the horn, your child woke crying, the dog went nuts.

Next time, coffee?

Bread Knife

Our bread knife had been missing for better than a month. Ikea had one with an asymmetrical wood and stainless handle that appealed to my inner Swede for only seven dollars. Where the original bread knife had gotten to was beyond my imagination, and below my cut-off for concern. Time passed, bagels were sliced and toasted, the new knife edged it's way into our daily lives. The transition was as smooth as buttering toast and we moved on.

On-line sources were not expansive enough for what I required. For reasons peculiar and picayune I decided one afternoon to use our old really big library style dictionary to look something up. "The first clergyman was the first rascal who met the first fool." was a quote from Voltaire but in what context? Who did he say it to? Was he just being clever, or was he making a point?

I needed the two thousand page dictionary to discover the truth. My discovery was very different. There was our old bread knife! It had been used (I don't know when) as a book mark. The entry "costumbrismo" was underlined. There was an old photograph (very wrinkled) that had been folded and refolded into quarters there as well. It was a sepia toned image of a chicken pulling a toddler in a little two wheeled wooden cart, and "Havana 1873" written on the back in florid script. Written down the book's margin in red was "Zarzuela" followed by four exclamation marks.

With my head buzzing full of 18th century French philosophy and 19th century Hispanic art I thought "I can make a cardboard scabbard for the old bread knife and seamlessly join it with gaffers tape to the black wooden block containing the new bread knife. Brilliant!" I was suddenly stunned by my entire lack of imagination. Given this sprawling mash-up of information and concepts in art and the humanities I was still mentally dealing with the bread knife!

Inaction would have been unacceptable. I refiled the errant bread knife under "R" in the dictionary to indicate both "redundant" and "resolved." I put the folded chicken cart picture in my wallet for another day.

Elvie

Well, huh.... Well, I'd have to say it was back when we were trying to be rodeo stars, say the second summer of the three. If you wasn't getting drunk every night and raising hell you'd be looking for something else to do so I started going to these services they got in the back of a big old storage trailer. The guy, Reverend Bob, or Pastor Joe, or whatever the jimmy cakes he called himself back then, would talk about leading a good life, a Christian life, just a life of doing right by others. The Golden Rule and all that. Not that campfire Jesus shit my Daddy always warned against, just being honest owning up to how you carry yourself in this life. So Bob would talk some and pray some, then maybe try and get a old time hymn going.

Remember this one time, well more than the one, somebody started in talking about this reincarnation business, how it was different than the resurrection of our Lord and a different thing too than all the saved folks rising up in the final days. Said you come back, but not as you was, or even close. Maybe as somebody else or an animal depending. There were a fair share of jokes about who'd be what, till I don't recall who took offense. Some of the boys liked the idea of a second chance at things, then one old hand pointed out us being runaway farm boys, rodeo trash, and day labor we'd do all the same stupid shit all over again.

So at these trailer prayer meeting, she'd be helping out. She was just a kid back then and this would have been late for her. I remember over her pajamas she wore an apron with twin Dutch girls holding watering cans. Her mother had some sympathies with what Reverend Bobby so she and her girl, the two of them, they'd ladle out pink lemonade while the good Reverend would call for a blessing from above. That lemonade hit the spot for sure, being hot in the trailer and all, but yeah, it was all them years back, the first time I saw my Elvie.

Curbside

The two of them were parked in front of the residential
YMCA, just around the corner from the hospital. A pair of
elderly gentlemen in motorized wheelchairs, both wearing
Run DMC '80s track suits, Nikes, and Yankees caps. Both
smoking cigarettes, tapping the ashes to the curb, pointedly
ignoring each other

Come Spring

our two old cats in spring
start their day black furred.
roll and squirm and wiggle
outside in the sunny yard.
by afternoon they are
covered in dusty pollen.
green as moon cheese.

Bus Station

The TV commercial confused me. There were beautiful young people in fluid choreographed motion. The dancing was perfectly timed, and their eyes were always connecting with the camera.

While in motion they unzipped pockets on themselves and each other. They coolly smiled goofy smiles, flirty smiles, knowing smiles so confident, and like magic, personal electronic devices popped from pockets, spun once, then grew on screen. It is unclear to me what these delightful youngsters were selling until a girl with a million dollar smile held up some twinkling plastic thing, and teasingly called out, "What's in your technology pocket?" "Oreos" I shout back in a splutter of crumbs.

Karaoke

Your sister and her friends were so drunk and loud, we were all told to leave the Karaoke bar.

Adamantly you insisting on doing one song before we left, and sang "What's New Pussy Cat" from the small and shabby stage.

You were horrible, and I never loved you more.

Safe Harbor

In Under Milk Wood,

Old Captain Cat, in his delirium, calls out;

"Let me shipwreck in your thighs."

For me, at age fifteen,

it carried such a sensual weight and power.

As a grown man it struck me

as both selfish and arrogant.

These days I find it speaks of redemption

and a loving forgiveness.

Man From Mars

Saturday I dropped a jar of pickles in the Dollar Store.

********** Breakage in isle whatever **********

High School girl at the register was very nice about it,
she smiled and told me, *Old people drop shit all the time!*
To make up for the mess I bought three jars
Quickly summoned a young lout carried them to my car.
To insure I didn't drop these too, I guess.
I wanted to give tip him, but only had a twenty,
so I shook his big doughy hand instead.
The boy looked at me like I was a fucking man from Mars.

Senior Momentum

So deal with my undergarments and pull up my pants.
Tuck in my shirt tails and do the button.
Fiddle with my belt and I'm done.
That's enough, I've lost interest.
The zipper can be for another day.

Crossing The Hudson

After her father died, I'd take the pickup to Westchester every Sunday and bring her a carton of Camels. Only family was allowed in locked wards, but the staff thought we were still married. Holding hands in the Day Room we'd talk and laugh for hours. When time came to go, we would kiss each other's eyes, it was our little custom.

Coming home I'd usually pull over to think, have a smoke, and watch the Hudson for awhile. Funny how things work out, you know. She'll still be locked in the Mental Hospital, and I'll still be in love.

ABOUT THE AUTHOR

Doug Mathewson writes short, and even shorter fiction. His work has appeared here and there, now and then due to the kindness and forgiving nature of numerous editors to whom he is most sincerely grateful. He is the editor of Blink-Ink www.blink-ink.org Also he sweeps up and does odd chores for The Mambo Academy of Kitty Wang.

More of his work can be found at Little 2 Say www.little2say.org